To Olly
Thanks to my editor Emily Ford
and to my designer Lorna Scobie.

Marta Altés is an award-winning writer and illustrator of children's books. Originally from Barcelona, Marta moved to the UK to study illustration and has since written and illustrated 8 picture books, winning the Ezra Jack Keats New Illustrator Honour, the Read it Again! Award and receiving three Kate Greenaway Medal nominations. Marta lives in London with a small dog called Sam. She also has a big, hairy dog called Floc who lives in Spain and looks suspiciously like the dog in this story.

First published 2020 by Macmillan Children's Books
an imprint of Pan Macmillan
The Smithson, 6 Briset Street, London EC1M 5NR
Associated companies throughout the world.
www.panmacmillan.com

ISBN: 978-1-5098-6604-5

Text and illustration copyright © Marta Altés 2020

The right of Marta Altés to be identified as the author and illustrator of this work
has been asserted by her in accordance with the Copyright, Designs and Patents Act 1988.

1 3 5 7 9 8 6 4 2

A CIP catalogue record for this book is available from the British Library.
Printed in Poland.

MARTA ALTÉS

NEW IN TOWN

MACMILLAN CHILDREN'S BOOKS

After a very long journey, I arrived in a very big town.

Everything was bright and exciting! I felt sure my new
home was somewhere here, I just needed to find it.

I started by asking the locals.

They seemed very helpful!

Although I didn't *always* understand their directions.

In no time at all I had seen
SO many places.

But nowhere that felt like
it was *my* home. Not yet.

I loved everything about that town.
The way it looked, the way it sounded.
Even the way it smelled!

But what I loved most were the people. Although
I must admit, at times they seemed quite strange.
We certainly did things differently.

But I always found them interesting.

With so many people around, I was
sure someone would help me.

But finding a new home was harder
than I thought it would be.

Everyone suddenly seemed so busy . . .

I realised that people didn't understand me.

Or really see me.

I felt a bit invisible. And so lonely.

But then something happened . . .

The little girl was lost and wanted to go home.

So I decided to help her.

We looked and we looked.

Little by little, I began to
feel less lonely.

Little by little, she began
to feel less lost.

Until she wasn't lost anymore!

She was happy to be home
and I was happy to have helped.

It was time for me to leave and find *my* home.
So I said goodbye.

But they didn't want me to go!
What I didn't realise then
was that I had already
found my home.

I've been here for a while now
and we still do things differently.

But each day I try something new . . .

and they do too.

We like it that way!

And that bright and exciting town
now feels like *my* town.

In fact, it's *our* town.
And it's home for **everyone!**